> Let every creature
> praise His holy name,
> forever and ever.
> –Psalm 145:21

For my neighbors, Hugh and Bethany.
With big thanks to Little Bear Noah, for the ark.

SIMON & SCHUSTER BOOKS FOR YOUNG READERS
An imprint of Simon & Schuster Children's Publishing Division
1230 Avenue of the Americas, New York, New York 10020
Illustrations copyright © 2007 by Tim Warnes
Scripture quotations taken from the Holy Bible,
New International Version. Copyright © 1973, 1978, 1984,
by International Bible Society. Used by permission.
All rights reserved, including the right of
reproduction in whole or in part in any form.
SIMON & SCHUSTER BOOKS FOR YOUNG READERS
is a trademark of Simon & Schuster, Inc.
Book design by Jessica Sonkin
The text for this book is set in Venetian.
Musical score arranged and prepared by Dan Sovak

Manufactured in China
10 9 8 7 6 5 4 3 2 1
Library of Congress Cataloging-in-Publication Data
Warnes, Tim.
Rise and shine! / illustrated by Tim Warnes.— 1st ed.
p. cm.
ISBN-13: 978-1-4169-1377-1
ISBN-10: 1-4169-1377-7
1. Noah's ark—Juvenile literature.
2. Noah (Biblical figure)—Juvenile literature.
3. Hymns, English—Juvenile literature. I. Title.
BS580.N6W37 2007
222'.1109505—dc22
2005020661

first
edition

Rise and Shine!

ILLUSTRATED BY *Tim Warnes*

Simon & Schuster Books for Young Readers

New York · London · Toronto · Sydney

Rise and shine
and give God the glory, glory,
children of the Lord.

The Lord said to Noah:
There's gonna be a floody, floody.
The Lord said to Noah:
There's gonna be a floody, floody.

Get those children out of the muddy, muddy,
children of the Lord.

The Lord told Noah
to build him an arky, arky.
The Lord told Noah
to build him an arky, arky.

Build it out of gopher barky, barky,
children of the Lord.

Rise and shine
and give God the glory, glory,
children of the Lord.

He called for the animals,
they came in by twosie, twosies.
He called for the animals,
they came in by twosie, twosies.
Elephants and kangaroosie, roosies,
children of the Lord.

It rained and it poured
for forty daysie, daysies.
It rained and it poured
for forty daysie, daysies.

Almost drove those animals crazy, crazy, children of the Lord.

Then Noah he sent out,
he sent out a dovey, dovey.
Noah he sent out,
he sent out a dovey, dovey.

Dovey said, "There's clear skies abovey-bovey," children of the Lord.

The sun came out and
it dried up the landy, landy.
The sun came out and
it dried up the landy, landy.

Everything was fine and dandy, dandy, children of the Lord.

Rise and shine
and give God the glory, glory,
children of the Lord.

That is the end of,
the end of my story, story.
That is the end of,
the end of my story, story.

Everything is hunky dory, dory,
children of the Lord.

Rise and Shine!

Rise___ and shine___ and give God the glo - ry, glo - ry.

Rise___ and shine___ and give God the glo - ry, glo - ry.

Rise and shine and give God the glo - ry, glo - ry,

Chil dren of the Lord.